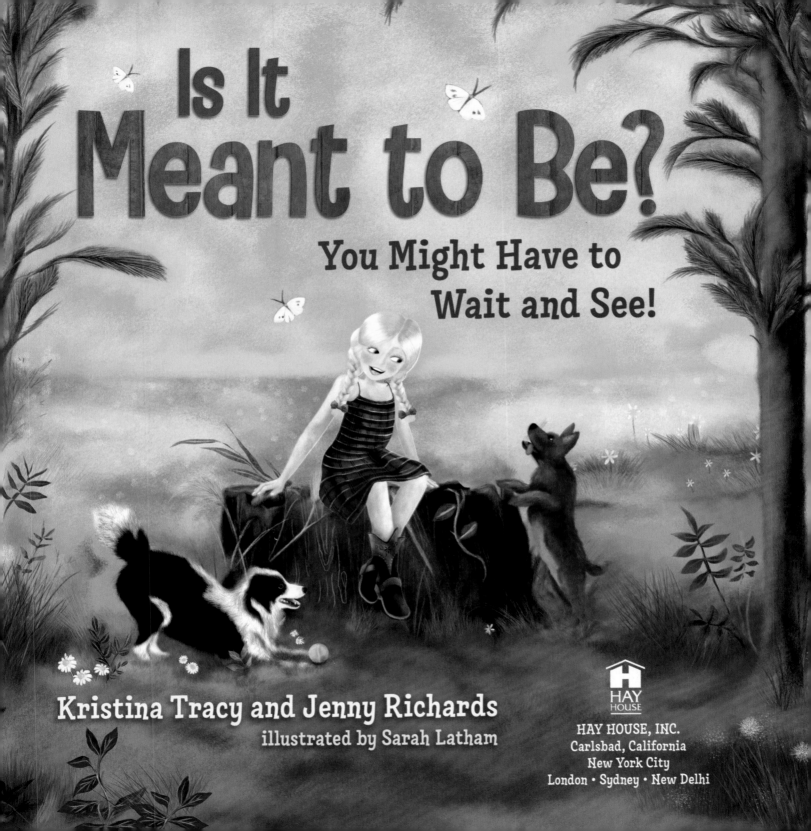

Is It Meant to Be?

You Might Have to Wait and See!

Kristina Tracy and Jenny Richards
illustrated by Sarah Latham

HAY HOUSE, INC.
Carlsbad, California
New York City
London • Sydney • New Delhi

Published in the United States by: Hay House, Inc.: www.hayhouse.com®
Published in Australia by: Hay House Australia Pty. Ltd.: www.hayhouse.com.au
Published in the United Kingdom by: Hay House UK, Ltd.: www.hayhouse.co.uk
Published in India by: Hay House Publishers India: www.hayhouse.co.in

Design: Jenny Richards · Illustrations: Sarah Latham

Library of Congress Control Number: 2021942204

Hardcover ISBN: 978-1-4019-6297-5
E-book ISBN: 978-1-4019-6298-2

10 9 8 7 6 5 4 3 2 1

1st edition, October 2021

Printed in the United States of America

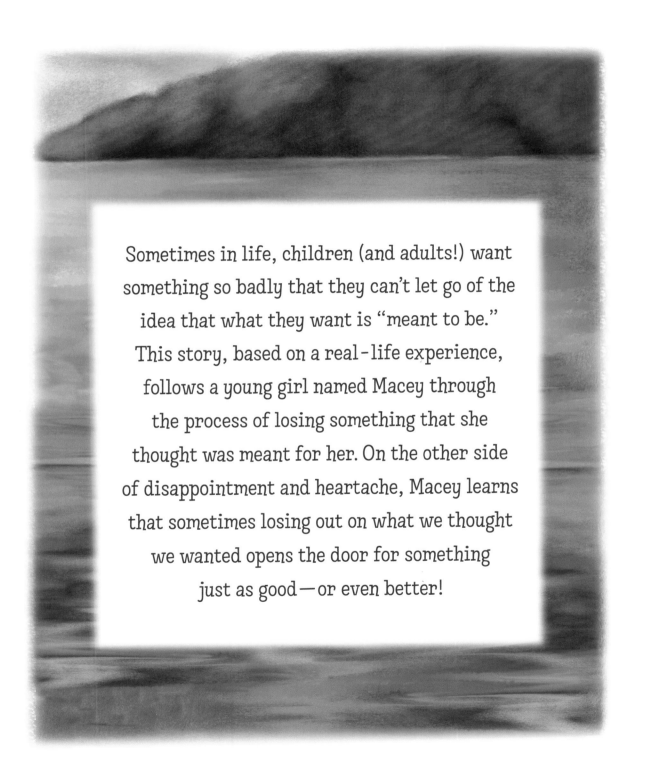

Sometimes in life, children (and adults!) want
something so badly that they can't let go of the
idea that what they want is "meant to be."
This story, based on a real-life experience,
follows a young girl named Macey through
the process of losing something that she
thought was meant for her. On the other side
of disappointment and heartache, Macey learns
that sometimes losing out on what we thought
we wanted opens the door for something
just as good—or even better!

One warm summer night, Macey was getting ready for bed when she heard barking coming from outside. She ran to her window and looked out. Macey and her family lived on a ranch, miles away from anyone and she didn't have a dog. So how could this be!?

It was hard to see, but in the light of the moon, she thought she saw a patch of white fur. She heard the barking again.

Macey ran and got her dad. "Dad! There's an animal outside! I think it's a dog!" she yelled as she dragged her dad toward the door.

When they got outside, sure enough, staring right at them, was a dog!
Macey reached out her hand for him to sniff. He was a little scared but seemed
friendly and he licked her fingers gently. Macey led the pup into the barn
where they could get a better look at him. He was skinny and dirty, but
Macey didn't care. She wrapped her arms around him in a big hug!
"It's ok, buddy. You're safe now!"

Macey stayed with the dog while her dad went inside to get food,
water, and blankets. Once her new friend was fed and tucked in safely,
Macey's dad said, "Ok, time to go back to bed. He will still be here in the
morning." Macey would have happily spent the night in the barn curled up
next to the dog, but knew that her dad would never agree to that!

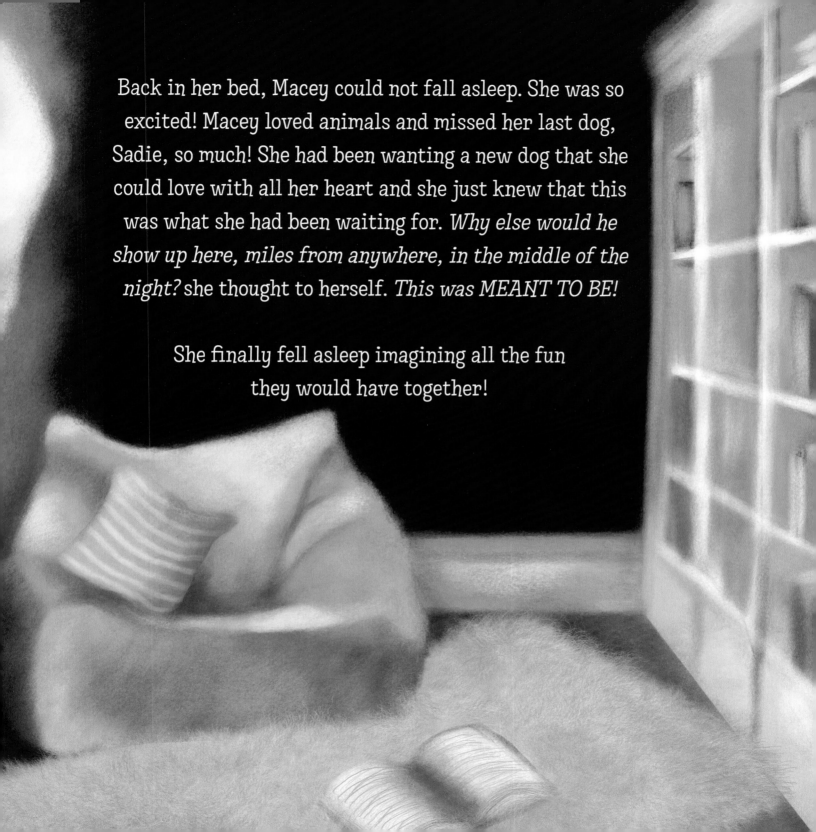

Back in her bed, Macey could not fall asleep. She was so excited! Macey loved animals and missed her last dog, Sadie, so much! She had been wanting a new dog that she could love with all her heart and she just knew that this was what she had been waiting for. *Why else would he show up here, miles from anywhere, in the middle of the night?* she thought to herself. *This was MEANT TO BE!*

She finally fell asleep imagining all the fun they would have together!

Early the next morning, Macey got dressed and ran out to the barn,
hoping it had not all been a dream. But there he was—
just as happy to see her as she was to see him!

She washed him, brushed him,
and took him into the house
where her mom and brother
were making breakfast.

"Mom!" Macey cried as she bounced around the kitchen.
"Look at our new dog! . . . Isn't he cute? . . . He is so sweet! . . .
Dad and I found him outside in the middle of the night! . . .
I love him so much! . . . I know he is meant to be our dog!"

"Wow, Macey, he is really cute!" her mom said.
"It would be great if we could keep him, but what if he's lost?
We will have to put some signs up around town in case
his family is looking for him. Try not to get too
attached to him until we know, ok?"

Macey agreed, but inside she was sure that he would be hers.

After breakfast, they made signs. As Macey drew, she decided she would name her dog Cap. She slipped him treats underneath the table and when she was done helping, they ran outside to play with him.

The next morning Macey went into town to put up the signs. No one they talked to had ever seen Cap around, but all the grown-ups said the same thing, "Don't get too attached to him." But it was too late!

The rest of the week
it seemed like Cap had
been their dog forever.
He rode around with Macey's
mom, kept her dad company
while he chopped wood,
and followed along on horse
rides with the family.

Macey could tell that she
was not the only one falling
in love with him.

When Cap had been with them for a week, Macey's mom came to her and said, "Sweetie, I have some hard news. I just got off the phone with Cap's owner. Her friend saw one of the signs we put up and called her.

"She said that when she was driving through town last week, Cap must have jumped out of the back of her horse trailer. She will be coming in a few days to get him. I'm so sorry, Macey, I know how much you love him. We all do."

Macey couldn't speak. She ran out the back door to the hayloft where she
cried and cried. She couldn't understand why this was happening!
Cap was meant to be her dog! Why else would he have come here?
Why did they have to make the signs?! This was so unfair!

A few days later, Macey and her dad met Cap's owner. He was happy to see her. Macey's dad asked, "Are you sure we can't keep him for you? He's already like part of the family. We would give him a great home."

"I'm sorry," she said. "He is my best cattle dog and he has a job to do on my ranch. Thank you so much for taking good care of him."

As Cap rode away, Macey's heart ached with sadness.
She asked her dad, "Why did this happen?" Her dad hugged her and
tried to explain. "Macey, it's hard to understand why some things happen,
especially when they are sad. Sometimes, when time has passed we can
look back and understand why. Hopefully, that will happen for you, but
we will have to wait and see. For now, let's go home and make some root
beer floats and try to cheer ourselves up a little."

As time went by, Macey started to feel a little better, but she still thought about Cap every single day. She wanted another dog, but she was waiting for the right one to appear, just like Cap had.

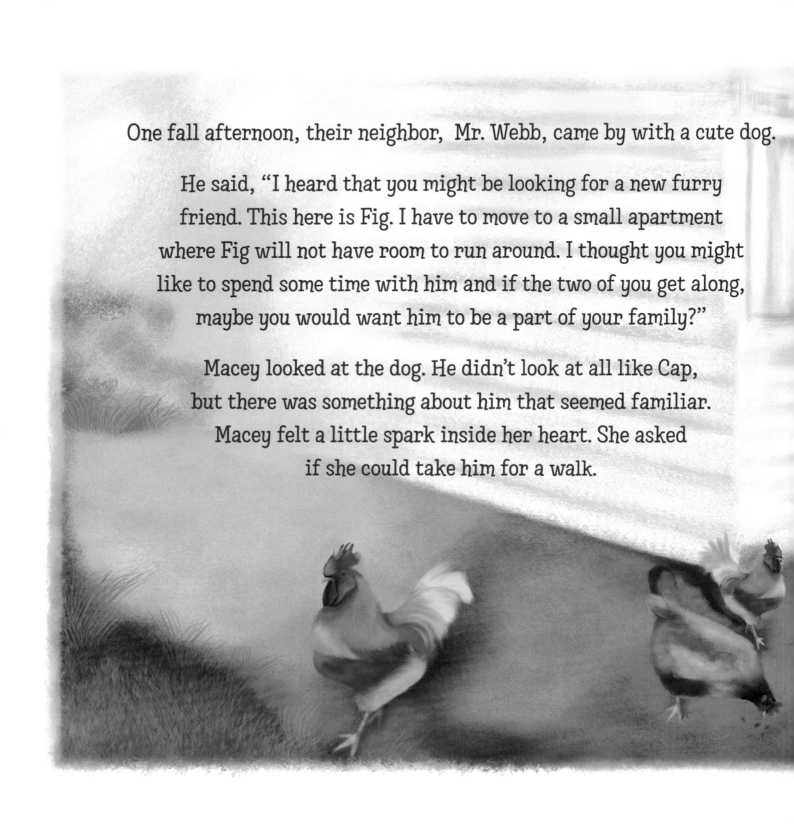

One fall afternoon, their neighbor, Mr. Webb, came by with a cute dog.

He said, "I heard that you might be looking for a new furry
friend. This here is Fig. I have to move to a small apartment
where Fig will not have room to run around. I thought you might
like to spend some time with him and if the two of you get along,
maybe you would want him to be a part of your family?"

Macey looked at the dog. He didn't look at all like Cap,
but there was something about him that seemed familiar.
Macey felt a little spark inside her heart. She asked
if she could take him for a walk.

Macey took Fig to her favorite place. She rubbed his ears while she thought. She was afraid to love another dog after losing Cap. But as Fig pressed against her, she knew she was ready to take that chance! Fig had come to her for a reason. He needed a home and she would give him a good one!

In her heart, there would always be a special place
just for Cap, but it was time to make room for Fig!
She ran back to the house to tell everyone the good news.

From that day on, Macey and Fig were always together.

Macey started to understand why things happened the way they had. If she could have kept Cap, then she wouldn't have Fig. And she couldn't imagine not having Fig! *Life is funny,* Macey thought. *Sometimes you think you know what's best for you. But you might have to wait and see what's REALLY meant to be.*

We hope you enjoyed this Hay House book. If you'd like to receive our online catalog featuring additional information on Hay House books and products, or if you'd like to find out more about theHay Foundation, please contact:

Hay House, Inc., P.O. Box 5100, Carlsbad, CA 92018-5100
(760) 431-7695 or (800) 654-5126
(760) 431-6948 (fax) or (800) 650-5115 (fax)
www.hayhouse.com® · www.hayfoundation.org

Published in Australia by: Hay House Australia Pty. Ltd.,
18/36 Ralph St., Alexandria NSW 2015
Phone: 612-9669-4299 · Fax: 612-9669-4144
www.hayhouse.com.au

Published in the United Kingdom by: Hay House UK, Ltd.,
The Sixth Floor, Watson House, 54 Baker Street, London W1U 7BU
Phone: +44 (0)20 3927 7290 · Fax: +44 (0)20 3927 7291
www.hayhouse.co.uk

Published in India by: Hay House Publishers India,
Muskaan Complex, Plot No. 3, B-2, Vasant Kunj, New Delhi 110 070
Phone: 91-11-4176-1620 · Fax: 91-11-4176-1630
www.hayhouse.co.in

Access New Knowledge.
Anytime. Anywhere.
Learn and evolve at your own pace
with the world's leading experts.
www.hayhouseU.com